Ready, Freddy! READER

SCHOLASTIC READER
LEVEL 2
250-750 WORDS

Caterpillars on the Move!

D0816354

by ABBY KLEIN

illustrated by JOHN McKINLEY

SCHOLASTIC INC.
New York   Toronto   London   Auckland
Sydney   Mexico City   New Delhi   Hong Kong

To Jody, an amazing friend who gave me the idea for this story.
Thanks for inspiring me!
—A.K.

For Mary Alice, with love.
—J.M.

ISBN: 978-0-545-14178-9

Text copyright © 2010 by Abby Klein
Illustrations copyright © 2010 by John McKinley

All rights reserved. Published by Scholastic Inc.
SCHOLASTIC and associated logos are trademarks and/or registered trademarks of Scholastic Inc.
Lexile is a registered trademark of MetaMetrics, Inc.

12 11 10 9 8 7 6 5 4 3 2 1   10 11 12 13 14 15/0

Printed in the U.S.A.   40
First printing, March 2010

Mrs. Wushy held a big box on her lap.
"I have a surprise for you," she said.

"Is it jewelry?" asked Chloe.

"Is it cupcakes?" asked Max.

"Is it candy?" I asked.

"It is something better," said Mrs. Wushy.

"Open the box!" we yelled.

Mrs. Wushy smiled. She opened the box very slowly.

"Eewww, yuck!" Chloe screamed.
"It's full of caterpillars!"

She ran to the other side of the room.

"I love caterpillars," said Robbie.

"Me, too," said Jessie. "They are so fuzzy and cute."

"Can I hold one?" I asked.

"Sure," said Mrs. Wushy.

Mrs. Wushy put a caterpillar in my hand.
It crawled up my arm.
"Ha, ha, ha! It tickles," I said.

"Can I have a turn?" asked Jessie.
The caterpillar crawled onto Jessie's hand.
"I wish I could take you home," she said.

"These caterpillars are going to be our class pets," said Mrs. Wushy.

"For the whole year?" asked Jessie.

"No, for two weeks," said Mrs. Wushy.

"Why only two weeks?" said Jessie.

"They are going to turn into something else," said Mrs. Wushy.

"I know! I know!" said Robbie. "Butterflies!"

Mrs. Wushy nodded. "Each caterpillar will make a chrysalis."

"What is a . . . kri-suh-liss?" I asked.

"It's like a cocoon," said Robbie.

"A caterpillar stays inside the chrysalis while it is changing," said Mrs. Wushy.

"What does it look like when it comes out?" asked Jessie.

"A beautiful orange butterfly!" said Mrs. Wushy.

We played with the caterpillars every day.
Jessie fed them lots of green leaves.
Robbie found them twigs to climb on.
The caterpillars got bigger and bigger and fatter and fatter.

One morning I ran over to the
caterpillar cage.

"Oh no!" I yelled.

"What is the matter?" asked Jessie.

"One of the caterpillars is missing!" I said.

"Let's look for him," said Mrs. Wushy.
"EEEK!" yelled Chloe.
She jumped up on a chair.

"What are you doing?" asked Mrs. Wushy.

"I am afraid of the caterpillar," said Chloe.

"You are such a scaredy-cat," said Max.

"Be nice, and help us look," said Mrs. Wushy.

Jessie looked in the sink.
No caterpillar.

Robbie looked in the crayon box.
No caterpillar.

I looked in the bookcase.
No caterpillar.

We looked and looked.

But we could not find the caterpillar.

A few days later, I went over to the caterpillar cage.

"Now all of the caterpillars are missing!" I yelled.

"Oh no!" said Robbie.

"Let me see," said Max.

"Where did they go?" asked Jessie.

"They are not missing," said Mrs. Wushy.
"They aren't?" I asked. "Where are they?"

"They are hanging from the top of the cage," said Mrs. Wushy.

"But I do not see them," said Jessie.

"Each one is resting inside its chrysalis," said Mrs. Wushy.

"Do you see that green pod?" asked
Mrs. Wushy.

"That is the chrysalis," said Robbie.

"Yes, that is the chrysalis," said Mrs.
Wushy. "Each caterpillar will stay inside one
for two weeks."

Robbie started to laugh.

"What is so funny?" I asked.

"I found the missing caterpillar,"
Robbie said.

He pointed to the ceiling.

We all looked up.

Right next to the light was a little green chrysalis.

"Will he be okay up there?" asked Jessie.
"He will be fine," said Mrs. Wushy.
"No one will touch him for the next two weeks."

Two weeks later we all ran into the classroom.

"Today is the day!" we yelled.

We looked inside the cage.

The butterflies had hatched overnight!

And the missing one was flying around the classroom.

Mrs. Wushy used a net to get it back into the cage.

"They are really pretty," said Chloe. "I don't know why I was scared."

"What are we going to do with them?" asked Robbie.

"Follow me," said Mrs. Wushy.

Mrs. Wushy carried the cage outside and opened the lid.

"Say good-bye," said Mrs. Wushy.

"Good-bye!" we yelled.

And then we watched the butterflies fly away into the sky.